To Theo and Nilo —P.M.

To Juana and Ulises —N.C.

Original title: *Nidos*
Edition copyright © by Kalandraka Editora, 2013
Text copyright © by Pepe Márquez, 2013
Illustrations copyright © by Natalia Colombo, 2013
Translation copyright © 2019 by Kane Press, Inc.

Publisher's Cataloging-in-Publication Data
Names: Márquez, Pepe, author. | Colombo, Natalia, 1971–, illustrator.
Title: Nests / by Pepe Márquez; illustrated by Natalia Colombo.
Description: New York, NY: StarBerry Books, an Imprint of Kane Press, Inc, 2019.
Summary: Each bird's unique nest is the perfect place to call home.
Identifiers: ISBN 9781635921267 | LCCN 2018954718
Subjects: LCSH: Birds–nests–Juvenile literature. | Birds–Juvenile literature. | Birds–Eggs–Juvenile literature. | CYAC: Birds–Nests. | Birds. | Birds–Eggs. |
BISAC: JUVENILE NONFICTION / Animals / Birds
Classification: LCC QL676.2 .M37 2019 | DDC 598–dc23

10 9 8 7 6 5 4 3 2 1

First published in the United States of America in 2019 by StarBerry Books, an imprint of Kane Press, Inc.
Printed in China
StarBerry Books is a registered trademark of Kane Press, Inc.

Book Design: Michelle Martinez

Visit us online at www.kanepress.com

 Like us on Facebook
facebook.com/kanepress

 Follow us on Twitter
@KanePress

nests

by Pepe Márquez
illustrated by Natalia Colombo

🍓 StarBerry Books
New York

In nature, there are many creatures.

Some live on land.

Some live in water.

And let's not forget about birds!

This is a bird.

tail

wing

feathers

other wing

eye

leg

beak

Birds come in all shapes and sizes.

And so do their nests!
Birds build nests to lay their eggs.

Every bird looks for the perfect spot to make a good nest.

And every nest is as special

as every bird.

Some birds build their nests in very high spots.

Others in low spots.

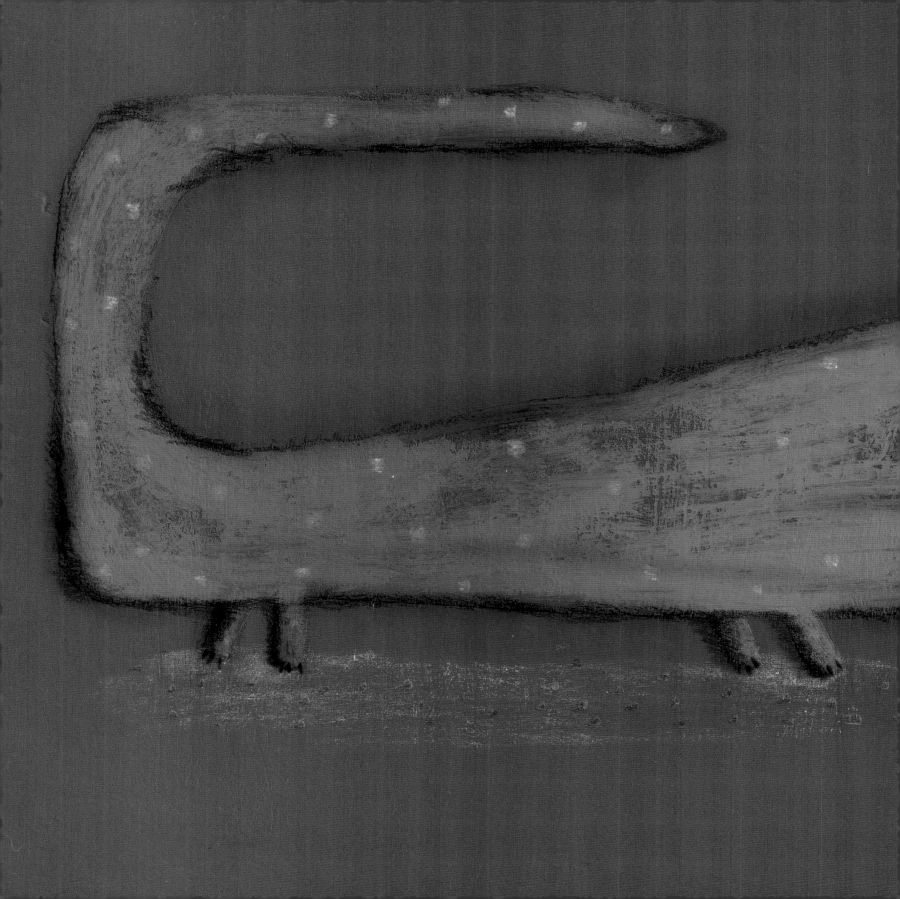

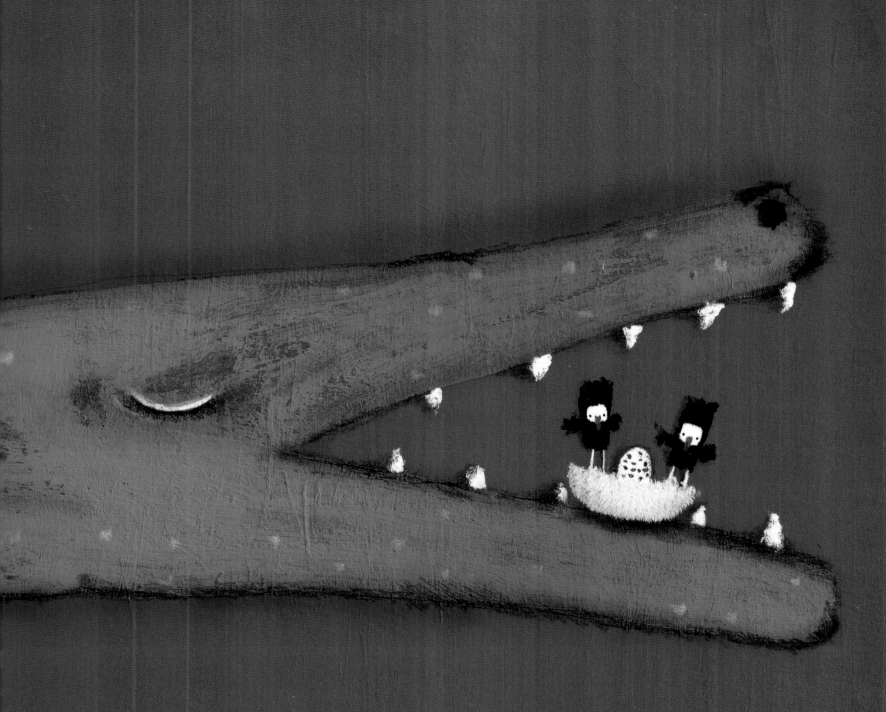

Some nests are in dangerous places.

Others are in protected places.

There are nests that feel small.

And others that feel crowded.

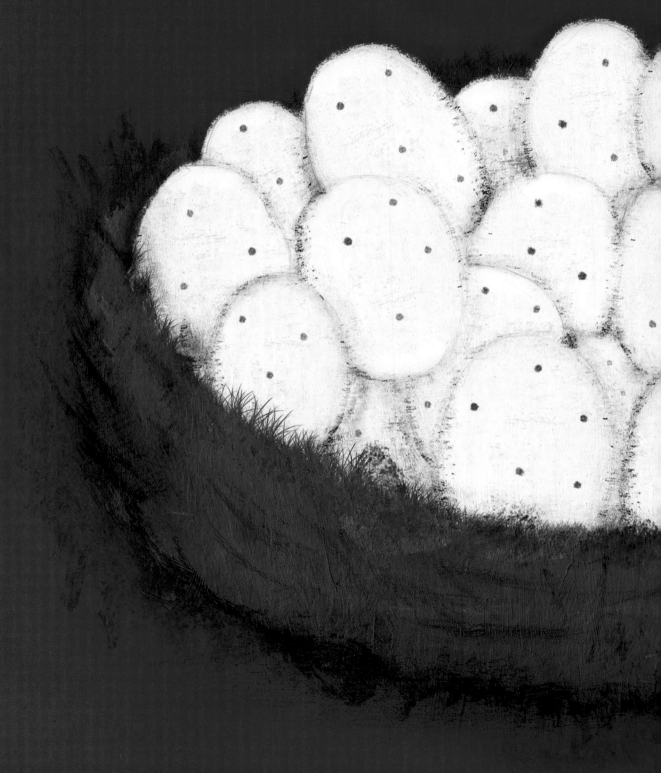

Sometimes a bird's nest isn't perfect.
Sometimes it's not in the best possible spot.

But for the bird family that calls it home . . .
it's the best nest in the world.